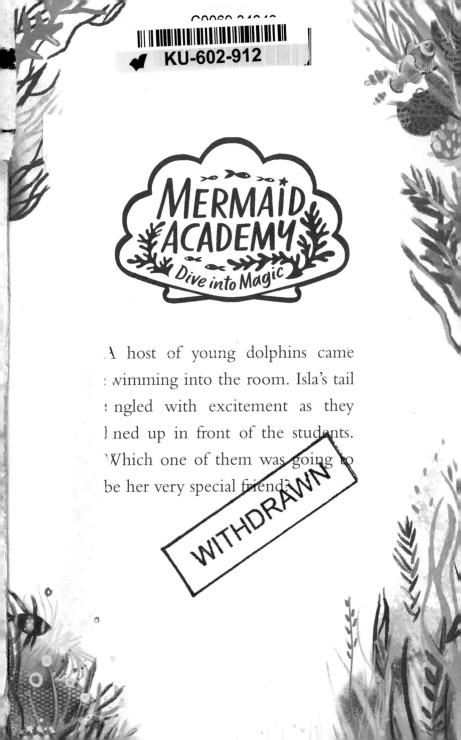

MERMAID ACADEMY
Dive into Magic

A host of young dolphins came swimming into the room. Isla's tail tingled with excitement as they lined up in front of the students. Which one of them was going to be her very special friend?

For the fin-tastic Kate Dummett
and Darwin Class

J.S. and L.C.

To Sybil, the sparkliest
little girl I know x

L.T.

MERMAID ACADEMY
Dive into Magic

Isla and Bubble

JULIE SYKES and
LINDA CHAPMAN

illustrated by
LUCY TRUMAN

nosy
crow

First published in the UK in 2023 by Nosy Crow Ltd
Wheat Wharf, 27a Shad Thames,
London, SE1 2XZ, UK

Nosy Crow Eireann Ltd
44 Orchard Grove, Kenmare,
Co Kerry, V93 FY22, Ireland

Nosy Crow and associated logos are trademarks
and/or registered trademarks of Nosy Crow Ltd

Text © Julie Sykes and Linda Chapman, 2023
Illustrations © Lucy Truman, 2023

The right of Julie Sykes, Linda Chapman and Lucy Truman to be
identified as the authors and illustrator of this work has been asserted.

ISBN: 978 1 83994 927 2

A CIP catalogue record for this book is available from the British Library

Printed and bound in Great Britain by Clays Ltd, Elcograf S.p.A.

Papers used by Nosy Crow are made from wood grown in sustainable forests.

MIX
Paper from
responsible sources
FSC
www.fsc.org
FSC® C018072

1 3 5 7 9 10 8 6 4 2

www.nosycrow.com

CHAPTER ONE

Isla whooshed out from the bubble tunnel in a frothy cloud of foam and gasped. The ocean here was much cooler than the ocean she'd just left behind!

Flicking her tail to keep warm, Isla tried to get her bearings. In the last few seconds, she'd travelled thousands of kilometres in the magical bubble tunnel her mum had created, and her head was spinning!

A strong current tugged at her and Isla felt her eyes drawn to the deep blue of the Wild Sea stretching endlessly behind her. Shivering,

she turned round and looked towards the crowd of mermaids and merboys heading through turquoise water towards a majestic coral building.

Mermaid Academy! she thought, gazing at the tall towers and turrets in awe.

At the end of a wide sand path, massive front doors were studded with barnacles, but none of the students were going in that way. Instead, they were swimming through an arch of pink coral that led into a large, round courtyard.

Isla and Bubble

Isla hardly ever felt shy but as she looked at the chattering, confident students she felt a flicker of anxiety. Mermaid Academy was going to be her new school for the next six years. She hoped that she'd make friends quickly and have lots of fun and adventures!

A ripple appeared in the water a few tail lengths away and another bubble tunnel appeared.

Two mermaids shot out of the tunnel. They looked identical, with thick, light-blue hair streaked with purple and green. Their tails were turquoise and they wore matching sparkly tops.

"Jumping jellyfish! It's even more beautiful than I thought it would be!" said one.

The other mermaid hesitated. "It's so big, Isobel," she said, her green eyes wide.

New girls, like me, thought Isla, her tummy twisting with excitement. She swam over.

"Hi! I'm Isla. I'm just starting here too."

The other girls smiled. "I'm Isobel and this is Cora," said the more confident twin. "Isn't it awesome being here? I've been dreaming about it ever since our invitation arrived."

"I almost didn't get mine," said Isla. "A Giganticus Whale accidentally swallowed the sailfish who delivers our post!"

"Was the sailfish OK? How did you get your invite back?" asked Isobel.

Isla grinned. "Luckily the whale let out a massive burp and blasted the sailfish out again!"

The twins both giggled.

"Ah, girls. Good to see you introducing yourselves," said a voice from behind them.

Looking round, they saw a mermaid with a smiley face and kind blue eyes. Her shoulder-length lilac and green hair was held back by a headband studded with tiny jewels. "I'm Ms Samphire, the Exploration teacher. You must be Isla, Isobel and Cora?" She checked their names off the scroll she was carrying. "Welcome to Mermaid Academy. It's almost time for assembly with our headteacher, Dr Oceania."

"Are the dolphins going to be there?" Isobel asked excitedly. "Will we get to meet them?"

Ms Samphire smiled. "Yes, and I promise they're just as keen to meet you. Now, please may I have your shell phones? They are allowed at the academy but not for the first week. We find students settle in better without them."

The mermaids handed her their shell phones.

Ms Samphire slipped them each into a labelled pouch and then put them into her bag. "Right then, get a swish on and follow me to the Grand Cavern!"

Isla's tummy fizzed with excitement. This was it! Her adventures at Mermaid Academy were about to begin!

CHAPTER TWO

Isla and the twins followed Ms Samphire under the coral arch and into a huge circular courtyard. In the centre was a jewelled golden harp on a pedestal. There were stone benches, large sea fans moving gently in the current and shoals of tiny rainbow fish swooping through the open windows of the buildings.

"We call this The Singing Circle," Ms Samphire told them. Isla thought it looked like a perfect place to hang out one afternoon, if she could summon the courage to ask the other mermaids to join her.

A group of students were gathered at the far side of the courtyard beside an entrance covered with a thick curtain of seaweed. Some were chatting; others were hanging back shyly. Ms Samphire took Isla, Cora and Isobel over and clapped her hands. "Time for assembly, everyone!"

A boy with black and pink hair put up his hand. "Will the dolphins be—"

"Yes, Arlo," Ms Samphire interrupted with a smile. "The dolphins will be there."

Isla and Bubble

Isla's tummy flipped with excitement. There was so much she was looking forward to – learning about the different oceans, training to be a guardian of the underwater world, discovering her own magic – but most of all she was looking forward to having her own special dolphin friend. In the first few days, every student chose a dolphin to pair up with and while they were at the academy they tried to bond. If that happened, they became partners for life.

Ms Samphire pulled back the curtain. "Enter the Grand Cavern!"

As the first-years swam inside, their chatter and laughter fell silent. The huge underwater cave was lit by flickering green sconces of mermaid fire. Twinkling bioluminescent algae dotted the ancient rock walls like little stars and there were beautiful mosaic pictures made out of tiny pieces of sea glass. In the centre of the cavern there was a platform with the biggest chair Isla had ever seen. It had a

back that was shaped like a whale's tail. Above the chair, suspended by an invisible force field, hung a globe of the underwater world with the names of the oceans and seas written in glittering dark-blue ink.

"Clattering clams! What's that?" said a merboy next to her with shoulder-length blue and yellow hair.

"It's the Magical Globe. It's an exact replica of our world," Isla whispered. Her mum had told her about the globe. "It can transport you anywhere you want to go in the oceans, no matter how deep or difficult the place is to find, and it's much faster than using a bubble tunnel. You have to ask a teacher's permission to use it but sometimes the globe will let you travel without permission if you've a good reason."

The boy gave a longing sigh. "I so want to use it."

Isla grinned. "Me too!"

Isla and Bubble

"Quiet now. Get into a line facing the stage, please, but leave some space in front of you," instructed Ms Samphire.

Isla got into line next to Isobel and Cora. More teachers filed into the room and formed a row behind the students. Hearing a sudden flurry of whispers and seeing a few of the first-years pointing, she followed their gaze to where bubbles were floating through a curtain made of shells at the front of the cavern. The opening bars of a song flooded out.

The curtain swished aside and a shoal of stripy diva fish shimmied out. Their red, yellow and green fins wiggled in time to the music and their high-pitched voices burbled along with it. A regal mermaid wearing a long purple cloak followed them, along with the biggest dolphin Isla had ever seen. *Dr Oceania and her dolphin, Crystal!*

The headteacher's black hair was streaked with gold and fixed in an elaborate bun decorated with tiny cowrie shells. Her gaze was welcoming but something about the firm set of her mouth made Isla quickly decide she never wanted to be told off by her.

Dr Oceania settled herself on the enormous chair with Crystal to the right of her. She broke into song, her voice clear and perfectly pitched:

"At Mermaid Academy we strive to be
The very best guardians of the sea.
With hearts that are true and open minds,
Let us keep the peace for all merkind."

The diva fish danced around Dr Oceania, their bubbly voices softly accompanying her melodious one.

As the final note drifted away, Dr Oceania

smiled. "Crystal and I welcome you to Mermaid Academy." Her eyes travelled the room, resting on every student. "Today is the start of your journey to becoming guardians of our beautiful world. The next six years will be a mixture of hard work and fun. You will learn about the many extraordinary environments we inhabit and how to care for them. The work will not always be easy but you have dedicated teachers here to help you. And, of course, you will also have the support of your dolphin."

Dr Oceania clapped her hands and a host of young dolphins came swimming into the room. There were big ones and small ones, bold ones waving their flippers and shy ones hiding behind the others. Isla's tail tingled with excitement as they lined up in front of the students. Which one of them was going to be her very special friend?

CHAPTER THREE

Dr Oceania's voice cut through the ripple of chatter and whistles. "Over the next two days, you and the dolphins will spend time together so that by tomorrow evening you can choose who you want to partner with at the Pairing Ceremony. At the ceremony you must promise to work together to try and bond. When bonding happens, the tips of your tail will change colour to match those of your dolphin."

Isla found her eyes drawn to a confident dolphin at the end of the row. His cheeks and tail fin were patterned with purple and yellow bubbles, stars

and swirls, and his wide mouth curved in a big smile. While most of the dolphins were gazing at Dr Oceania, this dolphin was prodding a smaller dolphin with one of his flippers. Isla watched curiously. The starry dolphin had a very cheeky twinkle in his eye. What was he up to?

She watched as he whispered in the other dolphin's ear.

The other dolphin giggled and whispered something back.

The first dolphin glanced at Dr Oceania and then, as the headteacher looked the other way, he opened his mouth and blew out a stream of tiny multicoloured bubbles. Isla smothered her laugh as they bounced along the other dolphins' heads, making them whistle in surprise.

Dr Oceania's head whipped round but by then the bubbles had all popped. The bubble-blowing dolphin gazed up at her innocently, his face attentive. Only Isla spotted the shake of his tail and the dolphin's next to him as they hid their laughter.

In that moment, Isla decided she really wanted to get to know the starry dolphin. *Look over here,* she willed him. But his eyes were now fixed on Dr Oceania as she announced which students would be in which dorm.

"You will sleep in your dorms and eat and have lessons with your dorm-mates," Dr Oceania explained. "There are six dorms with four students in each. Girls are in Moon Pearl, Lilac Star and Ocean Mist, and boys in Sea Jet, Sun Garnet and Midnight Diamond."

Dr Oceania produced a scroll and began to read: "In Moon Pearl are Maya, Amber, Isla and Cora."

Turning to smile at the twins, Isla saw that Cora's face had crumpled in dismay and she was whispering to Isobel.

"Don't be a dozy dory, Cor," Isobel loudly whispered back. "We'll still see each other lots even if we're in different dorms. And making new friends will be fun!"

Cora didn't look convinced. Isla sent her a comforting smile, but she also found herself secretly hoping that Maya and Amber would turn out to be a bit more outgoing and less timid. She really wanted some friends who were fun and adventurous. She looked around, wondering who they were.

Dr Oceania read out the rest of the dorms then clapped her hands to quieten the excited chattering. "There will be no lessons for the first two days of term. Instead each dorm will be given a list of things

18

to find in the school grounds. This will give you a chance to explore the school while getting to know your dorm-mates. Ten sea-star points will be awarded to the winning dorm and each team that finds everything on their list will get five sea stars."

Isla felt a rush of excitement – she loved treasure hunts!

The boy she had spoken to earlier put up his hand. "Can dolphins join our treasure-hunting teams?"

Dr Oceania nodded. "Yes, Obasi. Use the treasure hunt as a way of getting to know them before choosing your dolphin partner for the Pairing Ceremony." She smiled round at them. "Now, off you swim and have some fun!"

CHAPTER FOUR

"Treasure-hunt lists, maps and collecting bags over here!" called Ms Samphire. "You must find the items within the school grounds. Beyond the school walls is strictly out of bounds. Lunch will be available in the playpark so please stop there when you get hungry."

Isla was torn between wanting to find her dorm-mates, Maya and Amber, and wanting to say hello to the cheeky dolphin who had been blowing bubbles. He was now surrounded by a group of giggling dolphins all begging him to teach them how to blow magical bubbles too.

Isla and Bubble

"I don't know how to teach you!" he was saying to them. "I've always been able to do it right from when I was a baby dolphin. That's why I'm called Bubble!"

Isla smiled. *He's so bright and bubbly*, she thought. *It's the perfect name for him.*

Bubble seemed to sense her gaze and turned to look at her. As their eyes met, Isla caught her breath. She'd never seen him before but somehow she felt as if she knew him. She couldn't explain it, but it was as though they were friends already.

Bubble swam over. "Hello," he said, his twinkling eyes searching hers. "I'm Bubble. Who are you?"

"Isla." She felt suddenly strangely shy. It seemed really important to her that he liked her. "I … I saw the magic bubbles you made earlier. They were brilliant!"

Bubble's eyes sparkled. "Rainbow dared me and I never say no to a dare."

"Me neither," said Isla.

They grinned at each other.

"Moon Pearl dorm!" A mermaid with long purple ringlets tied up in a pony tail waved a list. "Moon Pearl! Over here!" She was with another mermaid whose raspberry-pink hair was in a long plait and who was talking to a dolphin with orange and pink lightning bolts on his sides.

Isla gave Bubble a hopeful look. "That's my team. Would you like to join us?"

"Definitely!" said Bubble flicking his tail.

Isla giggled. "That's fantastic! Come on then!" They raced over to the two mermaids. "Hi, I'm Isla and this is Bubble," said Isla. "He's going to be on our team."

The mermaid holding the list smiled. "Great. The more help we have the better. I'm Maya."

"And I'm Amber and this is Flash," said Amber, nodding to the dolphin next to her. "He's offered

to help us too."

"I like competitions!" said Flash.

"Me too," said Amber. "My favourite subject is games. I love fin-ball."

"That's my favourite game too!" said Flash.

"So what do we need to find?" Isla asked eagerly.

Maya read out the list. "An empty fish-egg purse, some Healfast seaweed and Knitbone

lavender, two different-coloured cowrie shells, a tuft of hair from a woolly seahorse, a prickly kelp apple and some pink sea moss."

"It doesn't sound too bad," said Isla. "Let's call Cora over here and get started!"

"Do you think we should get another dolphin to help us first?" said Maya.

Isla noticed her eyes straying towards the dolphin who had been next to Bubble in the line. The little dolphin was prancing around, wearing a clump of seaweed on her head as if it was a hat. Isla nudged Bubble. "Bubble, you know that dolphin, don't you?"

Bubble nodded. "That's Rainbow. She's really friendly."

"Should we ask her if she'd like to join us?" suggested Isla.

"Oh, yes!" Maya said so eagerly that Isla wondered if she had the same kind of feelings about Rainbow that she'd had when she'd first seen Bubble.

"Why don't *you* ask her?" she said.

Maya looked uncertain. "Me? But she doesn't know me."

"So? Bubble didn't know me," said Isla.

Maya hesitated but then nodded. "OK." She swam over to Rainbow. "Hi, I'm er … Maya. I was wondering … would… Would you like to help my team?"

The seaweed hat slipped over one of Rainbow's eyes. She looked solemnly at Maya with the other and shook her head. "Nope."

Maya's face turned redder than a sea tomato. "Oh. OK." She turned round hastily and started swimming back to the others.

The little dolphin giggled and chased after her, swooshing up in front of her.

"Just squidding!" She poked Maya with one of her fins, making Maya squeak in surprise. "I'd love to help you!" Maya looked taken aback for a moment but then smiled.

Rainbow raced over to Bubble. "Hey, Bubble! We're on the same team! How swishy is that!" They bumped noses and then Flash introduced himself too.

"This is brilliant," said Isla happily. "Three of us and three dolphins. I'll go and fetch Cora." She swam over to where Cora was hovering near Isobel and the mermaids in Ocean Mist dorm. "Cora! Are you coming?"

Cora looked torn.

Isla and Bubble

Isobel glanced at her. "You go, Cora. We'll see each other later." She turned back to her new dorm-mates and carried on chatting.

Isla saw Cora's face fall. She was about to try and comfort her but a pretty light-blue dolphin beat her to it. "Hi, I'm Sparkle," she said, swimming up to Cora. "I haven't got a team yet. Can I go with you?" She pushed her head under Cora's arm.

Cora managed a small smile. "Sure."

"Great!" said Sparkle happily, and Isla saw Cora's smile widen.

Sorted, Isla thought in relief. *Four mermaids and four dolphins. We're ready to go!*

They swam back to the others and Sparkle and Cora introduced themselves.

Maya unrolled the map. "OK, let's work out where to go."

"Or we could just start swimming and see where we end up," said Bubble.

Isla could tell she and Bubble were going to get along. "I think that's a much better idea!" she exclaimed, swimming across the courtyard. "Come on, Moon Pearl. It's treasure hunt time!"

CHAPTER FIVE

With a whoop, Amber joined Isla, and a second later Bubble and Flash had caught up with them.

"Wait! We don't know where we're going," called Maya.

"So?" Isla cried. "Let's just explore!"

She pointed at a signpost with an arrow and a label saying "Kitchen Garden". "I bet there are some prickly kelp apples in the kitchen garden. How about we try there?" She grinned at Amber. "Last one there is a slimy sea squirt!"

"You'll never beat me!" said Amber, her tail flicking rapidly as she powered away through the water.

"Take hold of my flipper," Bubble urged Isla. "We'll be faster that way."

Isla was thrilled. Merpeople and dolphins could share their energy and swim super-fast by touching flipper or fin to hand, but they usually only did that when they were officially paired together.

Reaching out for Bubble's fin, she felt a burst of energy zap through her that made her tail tingle and sparkle. The rush propelled them through

the water. She'd never swum so fast! They easily overtook Amber and Flash and reached the kitchen garden first.

"We won!" Isla cried, high-fiving Bubble.

"You were really quick!" panted Amber, as she and Flash swooshed up next to them. "How did you go so fast? Did you combine energy?"

"We did," said Isla, smiling at Bubble, who blew a single happy bubble at her.

"Next time we'll combine our energy too," Flash said to Amber. "Then I bet we'll win."

Amber grinned. "Cool. Should we wait for the others or shall we go into the garden?" she asked Isla.

Looking into the kitchen garden with its raised beds of sea vegetables, Isla could see the Sea Jet boys – Arlo, Obasi, Nimesh and Seb – clustered around a kelp apple tree. The small, sweet apples were nestling right by the trunk, protected by a

mass of long, sharp spines on the branches.

"I think we should go in," she said to Amber.

They headed for the tree.

"Arlo! Arlo!" the boys were chanting. Arlo wormed his arm between the spines and plucked one of the little pink apples.

"Got it!" he said, carefully withdrawing his arm. He grinned at the girls. "Bet you can't pick one, Moon Pearl!"

"Oh, really?" said Isla.

"Go, Isla!" whistled Bubble. "You can do it!"

Spurred on by Bubble's encouragement, Isla plunged her hand into the tree and immediately stabbed herself on one of the spiny thorns. She

yelped and pulled her hand out.

"Are you OK?" said Obasi.

"Yes, I'm fine," Isla said, sucking her injured finger. It hurt but she wasn't going to admit it.

"Try again!" Bubble urged.

"Good luck!" said Arlo. "We're off to find some cowrie shells!"

The boys raced off.

Isla had another go at grabbing a prickly kelp apple but once again the branches stabbed her. She squealed and pulled her hand out just as Maya and Cora came swimming up.

"Isla, be careful!" said Maya in alarm.

Isla exclaimed in frustration. "These apples are impossible to get!"

"I've picked kelp apples before," said Cora. "Let me try."

She waited patiently for the branches to sway to one side in the current and then carefully reached

in and plucked an apple without getting a single scratch. "Got one!" she said, handing it to Maya.

"That was brilliant," said Amber.

"Yes, well done, Cora," said Maya.

Isla smarted slightly. *I'd have got one if I'd gone more slowly.* The trouble was, she never liked doing anything slowly! But she didn't want her new dorm-mates to think badly of her so she smiled at Cora. "You did really well. So where should we go next?"

"I think we'll find Knitbone and Healfast in the medicinal beds," said Amber, pointing across the kitchen gardens to where there were some separate long raised beds of herbs planted in neat rows.

They set off. Each bed of medicinal herbs had a driftwood sign but the writing was tiny and hard to read. Isla, Maya and Cora swam slowly, reading each one.

"This is going to take ages!" said Isla impatiently.

"Here!" said Amber, suddenly whooshing up in front of them with two handfuls of herbs. "Healfast and Knitbone!"

"How did you find them so quickly?" Maya said, astonished.

Amber shrugged. "My older sisters are at school here and mer-medicine is their favourite class. Last holiday, they insisted on telling me all about medicinal herbs, and I've got a pretty good memory."

Flash spun round. "That's two more things to tick off the list. We're doing really well. I hope we win!"

And I hope I can win the next object for us, thought Isla.

CHAPTER
SIX

They swam on and reached a place called the Tranquillity Haven. It was very peaceful. Wind chimes hung from the coral, shell paths wound between marble statues and there were pretty rock displays covered in anemones. Bubble was delighted when he found a pink cowrie shell on one of the paths and then Rainbow found a lilac cowrie at the base of a statue of a wise merman. She bobbed over, giggling as she balanced it on the end of her nose, and then tossed it at Maya. "Catch!"

"Rainbow, be careful!" Maya gasped as the shell plummeted towards a deep crack in a rock. Amber

threw herself through
the water and grabbed
it just in time.

"Got it!" she said in relief.

"Whoops! Sorry!" said Rainbow.

"Good save, Amber!" said Flash, high-fiving
her with his flipper.

"Let's keep going!" urged Bubble.

Maya found an empty fish-egg purse near some
brain coral and then Isla spotted some pink sea
moss on the woven fence around the playpark. As
she untangled it, happy shrieks of laughter floated
towards her. She looked over the top of the fence.
The playpark was full of first-years having fun:
riding the spinning clams, whizzing down the
spiral mother-of-pearl slides and bouncing on
giant sponge trampolines. A picnic table had
been set with plates of seaweed wraps and bowls
of kelp crisps.

"There's Isobel!" Cora exclaimed in delight.

"Shall we go in?" said Amber.

"Yes, let's!" said Isla eagerly. "It looks awesome."

"But what about the treasure hunt?" protested Maya.

"Flippers to that! Let's have some fun!" said Bubble, leaping over the fence.

Laughing, Isla charged after him and the rest of the dorm followed. When they were too tired to play any more, they got some lunch and sat down on the giant sponges. Cora took her food over to where Isobel was eating with her dorm.

The rest of Moon Pearl chatted while they ate, sharing stories of the oceans they had come from.

"It's warmer where I live," said Isla. "The cold water was a shock at first but I'm getting used to it."

"Me too," Amber agreed. "Swiftail's ocean is warmer and more peaceful. The currents here

are exhausting."

"I like it," said Maya. "It's a lot like home but with different plants and fish."

Amber finished her second seaweed wrap and flopped back on the sponge, her hands behind her head, and sighed contentedly. "I could stay here all day!"

"But we need to get on with the treasure hunt," said Maya.

Isla pulled Amber up. "Maya's right. Come on, you lazy lobster!" she said. "We only need to find a woolly seahorse and then we've won!" She looked round. "Cora! Time to go!"

Cora reluctantly left Isobel's side.

"I think we should try the wildlife reef," said Maya, who had been studying the map. "It sounds like the kind of place where we might find a woolly seahorse."

"Cool," said Isla. A wildlife reef sounded fun!

"Woolly seahorses do like coral reefs," said Amber.

"Then what are we waiting for?" said Bubble eagerly. "Let's go!"

It was a long swim but when they got there Isla thought it was definitely worth the effort. The colourful reef was teeming with life. There were manta rays swooping along, trumpet fish bobbing upside down as they searched for food, spiny lobsters picking their way through the coral, and shoals of translucent glass fish that swirled around them before streaming away. The one thing they didn't see was a woolly seahorse.

"This is really odd," said Amber, mystified. "I'm sure my sisters told me there was a family of them here."

Rainbow chuckled. "They probably heard that the new students are going to take all their fur and have gone into hiding!"

They grinned.

"Let's keep looking!" said Isla.

They swam on, stopping only when they reached the purple boundary wall, made from moon rock and star coral, that separated the academy from the wild sea beyond. The water outside the grounds seemed deeper and darker, and there was a mysterious forest of tall red and orange sea firs stretching away as far as she could see. It looked scary but also exciting.

"I'd like to explore in there," said Isla.

"Me too," said Bubble eagerly.

She grinned at him. She might not have known him for long but already she was sure he was the dolphin she wanted to pair with. They were so alike!

"We're not allowed out of the school grounds," Maya said. "The forest's really dangerous. There's a crevasse in it that leads all the way down to the Abyss, the deepest part of the ocean, and if you swim too close it sucks you in."

They all shivered.

"I know it's dangerous but I don't mind taking a quick look," said Isla. "There might be some woolly seahorses out there." She glanced at Bubble. "Bubble and I could go together?" Bubble nodded excitedly.

"No, Isla!" Maya said swiftly. "You mustn't leave the grounds."

"Please don't go," said Cora anxiously.

Isla frowned in frustration. "But we've looked everywhere else."

"I know!" Amber said. "How about we ask the Sea Sphinx? She might tell us where all the woolly seahorses have gone."

Isla had heard about the Sea Sphinx: a wise, living statue that was half mermaid, half octopus, who could answer any question – if she wanted to.

"Do you think she'll answer us?" said Maya doubtfully.

Amber grinned. "There's only one way to find out!"

CHAPTER SEVEN

The Sea Sphinx statue stood in the centre of a small maze. The floor around her was covered with a carpet of beautiful white anemones.

"Whoa!" Isla breathed, as they stared at the huge statue. "She's massive!" The sphinx towered over them, a giant figure of midnight-blue stone that shimmered with green, blue and yellow flecks. Her head was bowed and her waist-length, copper-coloured locs were crowned with a shell-studded tiara. From the waist down, her body was that of an octopus with eight differently coloured legs, each patterned with stars and

moons that glowed in the semi-darkness. *She's so majestic…* Isla thought. *But also terrifying!*

"She's beautiful," breathed Maya.

"Shall I ask her about the seahorses?" said Isla. The others nodded. Isla took a breath and ventured forward with Bubble beside her. "Um… Hi there," she said, unsure how to address the statue. "Please can you tell us where to find a woolly seahorse?"

The sphinx didn't reply. Isla was about to ask again when the sphinx lifted her head and looked straight at her with her stone eyes.

Isla felt like turning and swimming away as fast as her tail would propel her.

"Ask again, Isla," Bubble urged.

Fighting her impulse to flee, Isla repeated her question. The Sea Sphinx continued to glare as if she wanted to squash her.

"This is freaky," Isla hissed, looking round at the others.

"Shall I try?" said Maya.

"Sure," said Isla.

Maya bowed her head respectfully. "Greetings, Great Sea Sphinx," she said politely. "We were wondering if you would be kind enough to help us with a problem. The woolly seahorses have all disappeared and we would like to know where they've gone."

The sphinx's eyes suddenly glowed bright blue. With a crunching sound, her lips began to move and in a grating voice she intoned:

"The situation's truly bad.
And one that makes me very sad.
Those who ravage and plunder our seas
Will never get any help from me.
But I am here for those who look
To rescue the things another took.
Travel quickly beyond the wall
To where the sea firs grow thick and tall."

A loud clunk rippled through the water. The sphinx's mouth snapped shut and the glow faded from her eyes.

"Clattering clams! What did that mean?" spluttered Amber.

"We could ask Isobel; she's brilliant at solving

riddles," Cora suggested.

"No," Isla said quickly. "We don't want her dorm to find a woolly seahorse first. Promise you won't say anything, Cora?"

"OK," Cora said reluctantly.

Isla thought about the sphinx's answer. "She said to travel 'beyond the wall' where 'sea firs grow thick and tall'. Do you think she meant the sea fir forest?"

"Well, even if she did, there's no way I'm swimming back there again today," said Amber. "It's ages since lunch and I'm hungry again!"

"I really don't think we should go into the forest," said Maya doubtfully. "Ms Samphire told us to stay in the school grounds."

"But what if that's the only place we'll find a seahorse?" said Isla in exasperation.

"Why don't we talk about it when we're back at school?" Cora suggested, edging towards the exit to the maze. "We could ask one of the teachers what we should do."

"Good plan," said Maya, joining her. "And if we go back now, we can find our dorm. I really want to see what it's like and unpack."

"Let's go then!" said Amber.

They all swam off.

Isla reluctantly followed them. "OK," she called. "But keep your eyes open for woolly seahorses on the way!"

CHAPTER EIGHT

When they arrived back at The Singing Circle, Bubble nudged Isla. "We need to go to the surface now."

Dolphins could swim underwater for ages but they had to surface occasionally to fill their lungs with oxygen.

"Does that mean we won't see you all until tomorrow?" Isla said, disappointed.

"Yes, unless —" For a moment Bubble looked almost shy — "you want to meet up after dinner?"

"Oh, yes!" said Isla, her heart leaping. She wasn't ready to say goodbye to him for the day.

Isla *and* Bubble

"We could meet at the bubble whirlpool and have a foam fight," Rainbow suggested.

Isla grinned. "That sounds brilliant!"

They said their goodbyes and the dolphins sped off. Isla waved the longest and before Bubble swam out of sight he waved back at her with one of his flippers, then he turned a somersault and raced after the others.

"Right, time to find Moon Pearl dorm," said Maya, running a hand through her curls, which were tangled from their swimming. "We need to unpack and tidy ourselves up. I read the school rules before I came here and students have to look smart at mealtimes."

"I'll see you at dinner. I'm going to look for Isobel," said Cora.

"What? Now?" said Isla in surprise. "But don't you want to see our dorm first?"

"I do." Cora looked torn then she sighed. "But

I want to see Isobel more."

"That's silly," said Amber bluntly.

Isla glanced at Amber in surprise. She'd been really cheerful all day but now she sounded grumpy. "Please stay with us," Isla said to Cora. At lunch, she'd noticed that Isobel had been so busy with her new friends that she'd hardly said a word to Cora. What if Cora went to find her and ended up getting hurt? "You'll see Isobel at dinner."

Just then there was the sound of a conch being blown. The booming sound echoed around the whole of the school.

"That's the dinner conch!" said Maya in dismay. "And we haven't tidied ourselves up."

"We could whizz to our dorm now," said Isla.

"No. I'm starving!" said Amber, folding her arms.

"If we go to the dorm, we might be late to

dinner and that could get us into even more trouble," said Maya. She glanced round. "Maybe we can find someone who has a comb we could borrow."

"Oh, Maya, stop fussing!" groaned Amber. "Let's just get some food!"

She swam over to where a crowd of students were swimming into the school through an arched doorway.

"I'm sure we'll be fine," Isla said to Maya. "Come on." She and Cora followed Amber and, after a moment's hesitation, Maya joined them.

A haughty student with long black hair streaked with green and gold was standing beside the doors ticking names off on a clipboard. As they got closer, they saw that a prefect badge was pinned to her sparkly vest top.

"Stop!" she said, holding her hand up as they reached her. "I'm Marianna and I'm in charge of

the dining hall today."
She spoke briskly.
"What dorm are
you all in?"

"Moon Pearl,"
Isla replied.

"First-years. Hmm,
I see." Mariana looked
them up and down and her
forehead creased into a frown. "Clearly none
of you have bothered to read the school rules
or you'd know that you have to be neat and
tidy at mealtimes." Maya's mouth opened
then shut as Marianna continued speaking.
"Since it's your first day I'll let you off, but if it
happens again, I'll give you a behaviour point.
I'll be keeping my eye on you, Moon Pearl.
This is not a good start." She motioned for
them to pass.

Isla and Bubble

"I told you we should have brushed our hair!" Maya whispered to Amber as they swam into the hall.

Amber gave her an irritated look. "Chill. It's not like she gave us a behaviour point and, anyway, behaviour points aren't that big a deal."

Maya's eyes widened. "Not that big a deal!" she repeated, her voice rising. "You might not care how the dorm does, Amber, but I do!"

Isla was about to try and calm things down when to her surprise Cora spoke up. "It is a big deal to get behaviour points, Amber. You know it is!" Her cheeks were flushed and her voice shook but she faced Amber squarely. "We should have listened to Maya and combed our hair before dinner." She glanced at Maya. "I'm sorry, Maya."

Isla gaped. She'd been under the impression that Cora wouldn't say boo to a sprat but she'd clearly got her wrong. Finding her voice she said,

"I'm sorry too." She nudged Amber and gave her a pointed look.

Amber sighed, the tension leaving her. "Sorry, Maya. Not getting behaviour points is important and I do want Moon Pearl to do well. I'm hungry, and when I'm hungry, I get grumpy." She grinned sheepishly. "My mum calls it getting *hangry*. I really am sorry. Friends again?"

To Isla's relief, Maya smiled too. "Yes, friends."

"Phew! Now can we go and eat?" said Amber. "I really am…"

"Starving!" they all finished for her and, giggling together, the argument forgotten, they swam to the food counter. It was piled high with bowls of delicious seaweed sausages and herby mash along with huge trays of kelp apple crumble for pudding and jugs of kelp fizz. The students ate at long tables and the room was lit by sconces full of crackling green mermaid fire. Paintings on giant reed scrolls of strange and wonderful sea creatures covered the walls.

They joined a table where Isobel's dorm were sitting along with the boys from Sea Jet. They were all chatting about the treasure hunt. Isla was relieved to hear that none of the other teams had found woolly seahorses either.

"It's such a mystery," said Maya. "How can they all have just disappeared?"

"I guess the first team to find one and get some wool wins the contest," said Arlo.

"That'll be us," declared Isla.

"No way, stingray!" said Arlo with a grin. "Sea Jet are definitely going to win!"

The talk turned to dolphins. Obasi and Nimesh had already chosen theirs – Arrow and Swift.

"I like Flash," Amber said. "How about you, Cora?"

Cora was so busy listening into Isobel's

conversation that she didn't answer.

"Maya?" asked Isla. "Have you decided yet?"

"I really like Rainbow," said Maya. "But it's a big decision. I don't want to rush into it and get it wrong."

"Well, I love Bubble," Isla said quickly, staking her claim in case anyone else got any ideas. "We get on brilliantly and I can't wait to see him later at the whirlpool."

Maya picked up her empty plate. "I'm looking forward to seeing Rainbow too but first, let's go and find our dorm!"

CHAPTER NINE

The dorms were all high up in the turrets of the school. Isla was the first to reach the Moon Pearl door. Pulling it open, she raced inside. "Whizzing whales!" she exclaimed. It was just as perfect as she'd hoped!

The walls were hung with strings of sparkly pink moon-pearl gems and there were four giant clamshell beds with pink and silver duvets. The top of each clamshell was decorated with glowing silver stars. Each girl also had a bedside table with a moon-pearl lamp that shone a bright pink. Along one wall were four cupboards for tops and

hoodies and jewellery, and four dressing tables.

Their luggage had been placed next to their clamshells.

"This is my bed," said Isla. "Oooh, it's lovely," she added, bouncing up and down on the springy sponge mattress.

Amber bounced on the mattress next to her. "Bet I can go higher than you!" she shouted, and they started having a bouncing competition.

Maya was on the other side of Isla. She began to unpack, taking out neatly folded tops and carrying them over to her cupboard.

Cora got some framed photos of her and Isobel out of her rucksack. She set them out on her bedside table along with a small silver flute. Isla noticed she looked a bit unhappy.

"Are you OK?" she asked.

Cora swallowed. "I guess. It just feels weird not being in the same room as Isobel. We've always

been together."

"You've got us now – your new dorm-sisters!" said Amber, overhearing.

"I know." Cora managed a smile but as she turned away to unpack her clothes, Isla saw the smile fade. *A distraction! That's what we need!* she thought.

"Hurry up, you two!" she said, stuffing her tops haphazardly into her drawers. "The dolphins will be wondering where we are!"

The thought of seeing the dolphins seemed to cheer Cora up and soon they were all ready to go.

The bubble whirlpool was a clamshell-shaped pool on the north side of the school. When the girls arrived, it was already busy with mermaids and dolphins. One half was swirling with warm water, which the students from warmer oceans preferred, while students from cold oceans dived happily into the half filled with cooler water.

Isla and Bubble

Bubble was playing with the other dolphins but he spotted Isla as soon as she arrived and raced towards her. "Isla!" he said, whooshing to a stop, his dark eyes shining with happiness. "I've missed you!"

Isla felt her heart swell like a balloon. *I should ask him to pair with me*, she thought. *Right now, before anyone else beats me to it.*

But just then Rainbow flicked a load of bubbles over them with her tail. "Foam fight time!" she whistled.

Flash and Sparkle charged over along with Amber, Maya and Cora and suddenly they were all throwing bubbles at each other and flicking them with their tails. It was great fun and they played until the bedtime conch sounded.

Marianna, the prefect from the dining hall, began to shoo them out of the water. "Time to go back to your dorms, everyone!" she ordered

bossily. "Half an hour and then it's lights out."
Her eyes fixed on Moon Pearl dorm. "Which
you'd know if you'd read the school rules!" she
said tartly.

They said goodnight to the dolphins. As they
headed to their dorm, Isla noticed the huge
marble statue of a mermaid at the highest point
of the school, lit up with a pale-pink light. "That's
a statue of Marina Star, isn't it?" she said.

They all stared up at the marble mermaid. She was holding a trident and resting her other hand on the back of a handsome dolphin.

"Yes, that's Marina Star," said Maya reverently. "The founder of the school. If it hadn't been for her, Mermaid Academy wouldn't exist."

Isla knew the story well. When Marina had been alive, the different mer clans had steered well clear of each other, all sticking to their own oceans. Marina had built the school to bring everyone together to share their knowledge and magic. The clans had been invited to send their young mermaids and merboys to train to be guardians of all the oceans in the underwater world. All the clans had agreed apart from one – the secretive Mal Mer, who lived in the Malmari Ocean.

"She was amazing, wasn't she!" said Isla.

"I'm so glad all the clans get on now," said Cora.

"Well, apart from the Mal Mer," said Amber.

Isla shivered. Her mum had told her the Mal Mer were very dangerous.

"My dad went into their ocean once to help an injured turtle. He told me it's like a wasteland there," Cora said. "They've taken everything beautiful and put it on display in their huge mansions, and they capture sea creatures like turtles and seahorses and keep them in glass cages just so they can look at them."

"That's horrible!" exclaimed Maya.

Looking up at the statue of Marina Star, Isla felt a rush of determination. When she was older, she was going to protect the underwater world and keep it beautiful for everyone to enjoy. An image of Bubble popped into her head. Would he be her partner?

Oh, I really hope so! she thought eagerly.

CHAPTER TEN

When Isla woke the next morning, she sat up and saw her new friends tucked up under their duvets. A wave of happiness swept over her. They had another exciting day ahead of them. There was the Pairing Ceremony in the evening and if they could just get a tuft of hair from a woolly seahorse then they might even win the treasure hunt! Remembering what the Sea Sphinx had said, a plan started to form in her mind.

She got dressed and swam down to the dining room, where she stuffed a bag with flaky seaweed pastries, urchin berries and drinks. Then she

returned to the dorm.

"Time to wake up, dozy dories!"

"Go away!" groaned Amber, pulling the duvet over her head.

"No. I've got a plan – and breakfast!" Isla held up her bag of goodies.

"Why have you brought breakfast to the dorm?" said Maya, rubbing her eyes.

"So that we don't waste any time. We're going to eat on our way to the boundary wall." Isla saw Maya's alarm. "It's OK, we're not going to go out of the grounds. We'll go up to the wall so we can watch out for woolly seahorses near the sea firs, like the Sphinx said. If we see one on the other side, we can try and get it to come to us."

"That's a great idea," said Maya, pushing back her duvet.

Isla glowed.

Isla and Bubble

As soon as the others were dressed, they headed to The Singing Circle. Bubble, Flash, Rainbow and Sparkle came racing over with Bubble in the lead.

"Isla!" he exclaimed in delight.

"Hi," she said, happiness rushing through her as he touched her nose with his. She decided she simply couldn't wait any longer. She had to ask him to pair with her. "Bubble, will you…"

He spoke at the same time. "Isla, will you…"

"Isla! Bubble! Quick!" Amber interrupted. "The Sea Jets are leaving. Let's go!"

Isla felt a surge of frustration. Now the moment had gone. *Never mind, I'll ask him later. Or maybe he'll ask me*, she thought, her heart flipping as she remembered that he'd been about to say something too.

As they swam to the boundary, the mermaids munched on pastries and Isla explained her plan to the dolphins.

"I might be able to help if we see one," said Bubble. "I can speak a little seahorse language."

Isla beamed at him. Her plan was going to work out perfectly – she just knew it!

At last they reached the boundary. They peered over the wall but there was no sign of seahorses in the shadowy sea firs.

After five minutes, Isla started to get impatient. "Come on, seahorses!"

"If only we had something to tempt them with," said Maya. "What do woolly seahorses like?"

"Sweet things," Amber said immediately.

"Why don't we put one of the leftover pastries on the wall?" suggested Cora. "If they smell it, they might come over."

"Good idea!" Isla took a pastry out of the bag. It was a bit squashed but hopefully that wouldn't matter too much. She put it on top of the wall.

They waited but no seahorses appeared.

Isla *and* Bubble

Isla had started to fidget again when Bubble nudged her with his nose. "Isla, over there!"

"A seahorse," said Isla in delight, as a small green and orange seahorse with a red fluffy coat and bright, intelligent eyes bobbed out of the trees.

"It's odd there's just one," said Amber frowning. "They usually swim in herds."

The seahorse came closer and then stopped, looking like it was ready to swim away at any moment.

"Hi," Isla called to it.

At the sound of her voice, the seahorse hid behind a tree.

"Flippers!" said Isla in surprise. "Why's it acting so scared?"

The seahorse peeped out.

"Let me talk to him," said Bubble. "Dolphins are allowed out of the school grounds."

Leaping over the wall, he approached the seahorse and talked to him by clicking his tongue. When he stopped there was a pause and then to Isla's delight the seahorse bobbed about. He spoke in squeaks to Bubble, his squeaks getting higher and more agitated. Bubble's eyes widened.

"What's he saying?" Isla called.

Bubble swung round. "I couldn't understand it all but I think something's happened to his herd. It sounded like they were captured or maybe they're stuck somewhere. Yes, that's probably it. No one would trap seahorses!"

"That's awful!" said Cora. "We need to help them." She dived over the wall.

"Cora!" said Maya, shocked. "You're out of bounds!"

"So? The rules don't matter if there are sea creatures in trouble," said Cora. "Who's coming with me?"

"Me!" Isla cried, diving after her. Amber, Flash, Sparkle and Rainbow followed like a shot.

Maya hesitated but then joined them. "You're right. If there are seahorses in trouble, we have to help," she said.

"Bubble, can you ask him to show us where his friends are?" Isla asked.

Bubble translated and the seahorse bobbed away.

"Stick together, everyone," Isla said, following him into the dark forest. "We're going in!"

Isla led the way, twisting through the sea firs. It was hard to see in the gloomy forest and fear prickled through her. Anything could be lurking in the shadows – viperfish, gulper eels, poisonous purple-ringed jellyfish...

She saw something small and round on the seabed and frowned. It looked like a prickly kelp apple. But what would a kelp apple be doing here? She spotted another. She was about to point them out to the others when the trees thinned out and they swam into a small clearing in front of a wall of rock.

Isla and Bubble

For a moment, Isla thought she saw a long dark tail slipping into the shadows of the firs – a mermaid? – but then she was distracted by a piercing icy tingle running through the scales of her tail.

"Creeping crabs! Does anyone else's tail feel odd?" said Amber.

"Yes. Mine," said Maya.

"I don't like it," said Cora, shivering.

The seahorse darted to the wall and back again. Isla could see there was a jagged opening that looked like the start of a tunnel. It was just wide enough for a mermaid to fit through. She swam closer. "Is this where your friends—" Before she could say "are", the little seahorse squeaked in alarm and shot in front of her, blocking her way. He bobbed up and down in front of her nose, shaking his head, squeaking very quickly.

"What's he saying?" Isla asked Bubble.

"He's talking so fast it's hard to understand but I think his friends are trapped through there," said Bubble.

"How?" Isla frowned. The tunnel was narrow for a mermaid but wide enough for a whole herd of woolly seahorses to swim down.

"It looks like there's something covering the opening at the other end," said Amber, peering round Isla.

Isla nodded. "I think it's a giant sea fan."

"If the seahorses swam in and then a sea fan fell over the tunnel opening, that could be why they can't get out," said Cora.

Isla nodded. A giant sea fan would be much too heavy for little seahorses to move and far too tough for them to swim through.

"Let's help them," she said, starting to swim towards the rock face. "I'm sure we'll be able to move it between us."

"SQUEAK!" The little seahorse zoomed in front of her again, stopping her from moving forward.

"It's OK, we can shift a sea fan," said Isla. "We've got hands and we're much bigger than you."

The seahorse continued squeaking.

"He really doesn't seem to want us to go any closer," said Maya cautiously. "Maybe we should stop and think about this."

"There's nothing to think about," Isla said impatiently. "We'll move it, free the seahorses, then pick up any shed fur and win the treasure hunt."

"But, Isla—" Maya started to say.

Isla interrupted her. "Stay here if you want but I'm going in!" Ignoring the frantically bobbing seahorse, she swam towards the tunnel opening with Bubble beside her.

"I'm with you!" said Amber.

"Me too!" said Cora.

"Oh, for Neptune's sake!" exclaimed Maya, but she followed as well.

Isla felt a rush of happiness. She loved having everyone follow her but as she reached the tunnel, a strong current caught her up and her happiness turned to alarm. She shrieked as she was swept inside and propelled along at lightning speed.

The sea fan! I'm going to crash into it!

Isla and Bubble

Isla braced herself but to her surprise, she didn't thump into the hard, fibrous sea fan. Instead it swung open just like a flap and she shot into a large cave.

Spinning round, she saw Bubble beside her. One by one, her friends and the other dolphins came hurtling into the cave. Maya was the last and as soon as she was through, the sea fan flap slammed down hard behind her.

For a moment, Isla was too shocked to speak. What had just happened?

There was a herd of woolly seahorses at the far side of the cave. They were clustered together, their eyes round with alarm as they stared at the mermaids and dolphins.

"Jumping jellyfish!" exclaimed Amber. "That was freaky!"

"Isla, are you OK?" Bubble asked breathlessly.

"Yes," said Isla. "What's going on with that tunnel though? It just sucked us in. I've never felt anything like that before." She swam closer to the frightened seahorses. "Please don't worry. We're not going to hurt you. We're going to move the sea fan and then you'll be able to—"

"Isla!" Hearing the alarm in Maya's voice, she turned.

Isla and Bubble

"What?"

Maya and Cora were trying to move the sea fan but it wasn't budging. Maya looked at Isla in fear. "We've swum into a trap!"

CHAPTER
TWELVE

Isla raced over to where Maya and Cora were pulling at the sea fan. "What do you mean, a trap?"

"I think that someone's fixed this here with magic to let creatures in but not let them out," said Maya.

"But that's impossible!" said Isla, shocked. "No one would make a trap!"

Maya pulled at the fan again. "Well, it seems someone has. It won't open from this side."

Cora gave a little gulp. "Now what? We're so far away from the school, no one will hear us if we call for help."

Isla and Bubble

"Stay calm, everyone," said Maya. "There has to be another way out."

Isla looked round, but apart from the herd of seahorses there was just bare rock in the cave. "There isn't." Guilt stabbed through her. She'd led her friends and all the dolphins into danger. "This is all my fault!" she exclaimed.

Maya swam over and put an arm round her shoulders. "No, it isn't. We all chose to follow you and it's good we did because now we can rescue the seahorses. We just need to stay calm and wait for someone to find us."

Maya's soothing voice helped to squash Isla's rising panic. *Maya's right*, she told herself. *When the teachers realise that we're missing they'll come looking for us. It might take a few days but we'll survive.* Then she looked at Bubble and realised something awful. The dolphins! They needed to breathe in fresh air each day. Without it they would die. Her heart plummeted like a stone.

"I think there's a magic spell on this sea fan door that means it only opens when something's coming from the other side," said Amber, who was investigating the flap.

"So if something else was to come through the tunnel it would open again?" said Maya.

"Yes, and if that happened, we might be able to escape, but how long do you think it will be before something else comes through the tunnel?" said Amber.

Cora gulped. "The forest was completely deserted." On the other side of the cave, the seahorses bobbed up and down in agitation.

"Poor things," said Amber. "They're really scared."

"I might be able to help," said Cora. She took her little flute out of her seaweed pouch. "The sea creatures near my home like it when I'm playing music." She blew into it and sweet notes flooded out. One by one, the woolly seahorses bobbed over. They perched on her arms and shoulders and a few even nestled in her hair, their little heads moving in time to the music. Cora broke off playing for a moment. "Don't worry, we'll get out somehow," she told them.

MERMAID ACADEMY

Isla wished she could be so sure. Swimming to a corner of the cave, she sat down, wrapping her arms around her tail. She'd led her friends into danger. How could she have been so stupid? She hadn't for a second thought that the tunnel might be a trap. Merfolk never trapped sea creatures unless it was to help them.

Apart from the Mal Mer, she thought, remembering the conversation she'd had with the others the day before. For a moment she thought about the shadowy figure she'd seen by the tunnel entrance. Could it have been one of the Mal Mer? But everyone knew the Mal Mer never left their own ocean.

Isla shook her head. *Focus,* she told herself. Right now, the only thing that mattered was how to get out before the dolphins needed air. She couldn't bear it if anything happened to Bubble and the others. *I bet he hates me now,* she thought miserably.

Isla and Bubble

If we do somehow miraculously get out of here, he'll never, ever agree to pairing with me.

She buried her face in her hands.

Suddenly she felt a nose nudging at her arm. Opening her eyes, she saw Bubble gazing at her. "Don't be sad, Isla. You did the right thing trying to help that little seahorse."

"Thanks, but…" Isla stopped and frowned. *The little seahorse.* He hadn't come through the tunnel with them. He was still on the other side. She remembered what Amber and Maya had been saying earlier and an idea started to form in her head.

"The seahorse who brought us here!" she exclaimed, bouncing upright. "If we could get him to come through the tunnel, then the flap would open. Then, if we could find a way to wedge it up, we could all escape!"

They all stared at her.

"But how would we get him to come through?" said Cora. "He didn't want to come anywhere near the tunnel."

"If his friends call him, he might listen," suggested Bubble. "I could try to explain to them what we need them to do."

"It's a good idea but it won't work," said Maya, looking round the empty cave. "There's nothing in here we can wedge the flap open with."

"If we grab the edge of the flap as it opens, we can hang on to it and let the dolphins escape," said Isla, not prepared to give up on her idea. "They could get help."

"But what if it's too strong for us to hold and shuts on one of us?" said Maya. "I think the magic helps it sense when a creature is coming, then it opens and slams shut the moment they're in the cave. It's too dangerous, Isla."

Isla's eyes prickled but she forced back her

Isla and Bubble

tears. All of their lives were in danger because of her. She'd let everyone down. If only she could make her plan work. In anger and frustration, she slapped her tail on the ground. "There's got to be something—" She broke off as a big pink bubble floated up from the floor.

"Jumping jellyfish, Isla! How did you do that?" Amber exclaimed.

"I... I don't know," said Isla, her eyes wide. She banged her tail down again and another pink bubble appeared, this time even bigger.

"It's your magic, Isla!" whistled Bubble. He danced round her. "You must have bubble magic!"

Isla gasped. Her older cousin, Lola, had bubble magic. She could create enormous clouds of bubbles whenever she wanted, or streams of bubbles powerful enough to send other merfolk head over tail. "Oh, wow," Isla breathed, for a moment forgetting they were trapped in the cave.

"Bubble magic is loads of fun! And look at my tail!"

When a mermaid found their magic, a symbol appeared in the scales on their tail. "I've got gold scales in the shape of a bubble."

"We can make bubbles together now, Isla!" said Bubble, blowing a stream of bubbles at her.

Isla slapped her tail down, picturing little bubbles

like the ones Bubble could make and immediately a cloud of them floated up to meet his.

Maya hugged her. "I can't believe you've discovered your magic already."

"It's fantastic!" said Amber, beaming.

"We've not even been at school two days," said Cora.

Her words brought Isla back with a bump. It was brilliant she'd found her magic and that she could make bubbles but it didn't change the fact that they were trapped and very soon the dolphins would need air.

"If only my magic was more useful," she said. "It's not like we can use bubbles to escape."

Bubble blew a jet of bubbles at her.

Isla gasped as the bubbles shot past her nose. "Wait," she exclaimed, zooming up into the water. "Maybe we can!"

CHAPTER THIRTEEN

"Ready?" Isla said, a few minutes later.

"Ready!" everyone chorused.

Her plan was simple and had come from the bubbles. What if they could trick the flap into staying open? Like Maya had said, the magic seemed to sense and respond to movement in the water. Her bubble magic was much stronger than Bubble's and it could cause a lot of movement. Isla carefully explained her idea and everyone agreed it was worth a try. Then Bubble communicated it to the seahorses.

Isla looked around. They were all in position.

Isla and Bubble

The seahorses were close to the flap, she and Bubble were to the left of it and everyone else was waiting hopefully in front.

"On the count of three," said Isla.

Bubble nudged her. "Hold my flipper. If we're connected to each other, then your magic will be stronger."

Isla took hold of his flipper. "One … two … THREE!"

The seahorses started calling to their friend who was still outside. Rainbow, Flash and Sparkle joined in too, whistling and clicking, encouraging the seahorse to come closer. Isla held her breath. Was this going to work? Would the little seahorse listen?

For a few awful seconds nothing happened, but then they heard the rushing sound of water.

"He must be coming!" gasped Maya.

"He's here!" cried Amber as the flap flew open.

Isla slapped her tail down hard as the little seahorse came whizzing through, carried on the magic current.

A jet of bubbles shot straight towards the opening. Isla gasped as she felt her bubbles hit the strong current coming in the opposite direction. For a moment, the water under the flap swirled wildly as her bubbles fought against the current coming in.

"Keep going, Isla!" whistled Bubble.

She gripped his fin, the energy zapping between them like it had done before in the race. Power surged through her, making every scale of her tail feel like it was sparkling. They could do this, they could!

Whoosh! Isla's bubbles won the battle with the current coming into the cave and they streamed out along the tunnel towards the forest. With all the movement going on beneath it, the flap stayed open.

"Go!" shouted Isla.

The seahorses and her friends needed no encouragement. They shot through the opening, carried out on the stream of bubbles. Maya and Rainbow were the last and Isla and Bubble dived after them.

Bang! The flap slammed down, missing the tips of Isla's tail by centimetres. She shot out into the clearing on the other side and felt her magic fade. The bubbles died to a trickle and, with a pop, disappeared completely.

"You did it!" Maya shrieked. "You and Bubble saved us all!"

"You're both amazing!" whooped Amber, as Rainbow, Sparkle and Flash somersaulted in delight.

"Look how happy the seahorses are," said Cora, as the herd nuzzled noses with the little seahorse who had been all on his own.

Bubble swam into Isla's arms and for a second the water swirled around them, making Isla's scales tingle. "You're the best, Isla. Your idea saved everyone."

As they pulled apart, Isla noticed her tail. The tips had changed colour. "We've bonded!" she squealed. "Look, Bubble. Our tails match!"

"Yippee! I knew we would!" Bubble blew a tiny bubble at Isla that landed on her nose. She giggled as they hugged again, wiggling their tails, showing off their perfectly matching violet and bright pink tail tips.

"Hoorah for Isla and Bubble!" Amber cheered.

When everyone had finished congratulating them, Isla's guilt came rushing back. "I really am sorry about what happened. It was my fault we got trapped. I promise I'll be more cautious from now on."

"Me too," said Bubble. "From now on, I'm going to think before I dive in."

Isla nodded and stroked him. "We're so alike. It's brilliant that we're partners but let's promise to help each other stay out of danger."

"I promise," he said, touching his nose to hers.

"And I promise too," she said, hugging him.

Maya grinned. "I'm not going to argue with you trying to be a bit more cautious from now on but you were both completely and utterly awesome just now. You saved us."

"And if we hadn't gone into that cave in the first place, the seahorses would still be trapped," said Cora.

The seahorses swirled around Isla and Bubble, squeaking loudly. Isla grinned. She couldn't speak seahorse but she didn't need Bubble to tell her that they were all saying thank you! The herd came together in a group and then zoomed away.

Isla and Bubble

The mermaids and dolphins followed them back to the boundary wall. The seahorses saw the pastry and with delighted squeaks they carried it away between them towards the wildlife reef.

"What I don't get is why all the seahorses went into the forest," said Amber as they all swam over the wall too. "Woolly seahorses usually live on coral reefs."

"It does seem a weird thing for them to have done," Maya agreed.

Isla remembered the sweet prickly kelp apples she'd seen earlier. She was about to tell the others about them when she heard a boy yell from the wildlife reef. "Woolly seahorses! Over here!" She was sure it was Arlo. "Come on, Sea Jets!"

She gasped as she realised something. "We forgot to get any wool!" She knew that saving the seahorses was far more important than winning the treasure hunt but it still seemed a bit unfair.

"Now the boys are going to win."

"Oh, no they're not," said Cora with a grin. "They've still got to get their wool but we've already got some."

Isla frowned. "No, we haven't."

Cora opened her hand and showed her a piece of red wool. "I got this when the seahorses were using me as a perch!"

Isla whooped. "Go, Moon Pearl! The race is on!"

CHAPTER FOURTEEN

"Well done, girls!" declared Dr Oceania after she had checked their collection of things. "You've found everything, you're the first team back and I see that Isla has already bonded with Bubble?"

Isla and Bubble nodded shyly.

Dr Oceania smiled. "Congratulations. That's very quick. It usually takes at least a week before a first-year student and a dolphin bond. And I can also declare Moon Pearl are the winners. Ten sea-star points for Moon Pearl!"

The four mermaids hugged each other in delight.

"So did you find the hunt useful?" Dr Oceania went on. "Do you know the school grounds better now?"

"Oh, yes," they chorused.

And we know something about the ocean beyond school too, Isla thought as her friends exchanged secret grins. They'd agreed that they wouldn't tell the teachers about their adventure in the sea fir forest. They didn't want to get into trouble for breaking school rules right at the start of term. Isla felt a bit uneasy keeping quiet about the magic trap, the prickly kelp apples and the shadowy figure she was sure she'd seen, but the important thing was that the seahorses were safe. And it was all because she and her new friends had worked together.

Glancing round at them, Isla suddenly realised that the adventure hadn't just taught her about the school grounds and the sea fir forest, it had also taught her a lot about her dorm-mates. *We're going to be a brilliant team!* she thought.

They swam off to share the massive bag of sea humbugs that Dr Oceania had given them with the dolphins. Isla's heart sang as Bubble swam up to her.

"So who else is ready to become a pair?" she asked.

"Me!" said Amber immediately. "Flash, will you be my dolphin partner?"

"Of course I will!" he said, his eyes sparkling. "I bet no one's going to be able to beat us in races when we combine our energy." Amber high-fived him.

Isla turned to Maya. "You next, Maya."

Rainbow looked at her hopefully but Maya bit her lip. "It's such a big decision. I don't want to rush…"

"Maya! Now's the time to be more like Isla," said Amber with a grin. "We all know who you want to ask."

"Rainbow! Rainbow!" chanted Isla, Cora, Bubble, Sparkle and Flash.

Maya grinned and flicked her tail at them.

"OK! OK!" she said, turning to the little dolphin. "Rainbow, please will you pair with me?"

Rainbow tilted her head and pretended to think. Maya's face fell. "Only squidding!" cried Rainbow, spinning round in front of her. "Yes, I will! I'd love to!" She kissed Maya on the nose and Maya beamed.

Sparkle swam up to Cora. "What about us? Will you be my pair, Cora?"

Cora looked torn. "I really want to but I think I should ask Isobel about it first."

"Oh no, you shouldn't," said Isla firmly. "Choosing who to pair with has to be your decision and yours alone. Go with your heart, Cora."

They all held their breath and then Cora's face split into a smile. "Then yes, please, Sparkle. I'd love to pair with you."

"Yippee!" shouted Sparkle, turning three happy somersaults one after the other.

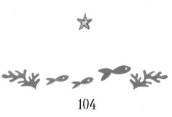

Isla and Bubble

That evening, instead of eating in the dining hall, there was a whole-school picnic. The courtyard was illuminated by thousands of glowing miniature squid that hung from the coral walls like stars. The first-year students and their dolphins gathered in the centre of The Singing Circle. Lastly, the teachers and older students formed a ring around them. Dr Oceania, carrying a golden conch filled with magic mermaid powder, swam up to the viewing platform and the statue of Marina Star. She raised it above her head and everyone started to sing, making the sea fans sway as the water swirled around them.

As the singing faded away, the prefects pressed their hands together to form an arch. One by one, the first-years and their dolphins swam under it, then up to Dr Oceania. There, under the wise gaze of the statue of Marina Star, they promised to work together to protect the underwater world.

Once each pair had made their vow, Dr Oceania sprinkled a handful of sparkling powder over their heads. The powder twirled in a cloud and then vanished, leaving each student and dolphin wearing a glittering seaweed crown.

The ceremony finished with each student receiving their own dorm-stone on a necklace and everyone singing the school song.

Afterwards, Isla sat with Cora, Maya and Amber, their arms around their dolphins. Isla sighed happily. She was so happy that she was in Moon Pearl dorm and that she had Bubble as her dolphin. Everything felt perfect.

But even as she thought that, a worrying image

rose up in her mind – a picture of a dark, sinister shape slipping silently through the sea firs and laying a trail of kelp apples on the forest floor…

Bubble nudged her with his nose. "Are you OK, Isla?"

She pushed the thought away. "Yes, I'm fine." She glanced down at both her and Bubble's newly coloured violet and pink tail. "More than fine," she said with a smile.

Bubble's eyes sparkled. "When we first met, you said you liked dares."

Isla nodded.

"Then I dare you to magic up some bubbles," he whispered, nodding at their friends.

"And I dare you to do the same," she whispered back.

A mischievous look passed between them, and in the exact same moment they shot a stream of bubbles at the other Moon Pearl mermaids and dolphins. Everyone squealed as the cloud of bubbles enveloped them before streaming upwards and forming a pink moon pearl over their heads. The exclamations of shock turned to laughter.

Isla and Bubble high-fived each other.

"Partners forever!" they both whooped in delight.